Thomas Holcroft

A Letter to the Right Honourable William Windham

on the intemperance and dangerous tendency of his public conduct

Thomas Holcroft

A Letter to the Right Honourable William Windham
on the intemperance and dangerous tendency of his public conduct

ISBN/EAN: 9783337194819

Printed in Europe, USA, Canada, Australia, Japan

Cover: Foto ©Andreas Hilbeck / pixelio.de

More available books at **www.hansebooks.com**

A

LETTER

TO THE

RIGHT HONOURABLE

WILLIAM WINDHAM,

ON THE

INTEMPERANCE AND DANGEROUS TEN-DENCY OF HIS PUBLIC CONDUCT.

By THOMAS HOLCROFT.

ADVERTISEMENT.

THE House of Commons, as one principal branch of the Legislature, assumes to
itself discretionary powers, among which
is that of calling to account those who infringe its privileges, or by-laws. To com-
ment, out of that House, on words
spoken by its Members, in debate, it has
thought proper to declare is an offence
deserving of punishment. I consider all
privileges as unjust; for a privilege sig-
nifies a partial law; a law by which one
man may profit, and another may not.
But, as I neither seek punishment nor
wish to incite men to commit injustice, I
would never wantonly act in opposition
to such mistakes. When, however, I
imagine I discover the means of benefitting
mankind, by opposing them, I then think
it an indispensible duty to disregard personal risk and erroneous institutions.
Being likewise one of those persons who
have acquired the last invented and newest
of titles, " acquitted Felons," it is a duty
that, in the present state of society and

the

the present instance, particularly regards me. Titles are become exceedingly equivocal, in their signification. In one country they are despised : in another they are sought with avidity, and bestowed with an insulting disregard to common sense and common decency. As far as the sound goes, I should be as little affronted at the title, " acquitted Felon," as flattered by that of my Lord, your Grace, or any other, which malice, fraud, or folly have invented. But, when either are to be construed as marks of approbation or blame, it becomes us to inquire into the merits of the case. The general result of such inquiries is a conviction that titles, like the contents of chapters in Romances, are frequently intended to mislead : and that, in bestowing them, men ought to be more cautious in their censure, and less profuse in their applause.

Newman-Street,
Jan. 16th, 1795.

A

LETTER

TO THE

RIGHT HONOURABLE

WILLIAM WINDHAM.

SIR,

THE Members of the House of Commons have
arrogated to themselves many customs and privileges; which they consider, some as rights to
indulge in parliamentary invective, and others as
limitations to those rights. Personalities affecting
Members of that House are contrary to order;
but men, unprotected by the sanctified walls of
Saint Stephen's Chapel, may be the objects of
assertions which, if made any where else, would
subject the authors of them to such correction
as the law affords; or as honour, half idiot
half demon, demands. For my own part, I
should never attempt to unsheath the sword of
the law, much less the sword of the assassin:
at least, if it were possible to oblige me to the
former, the case must indeed be extreme.
Under such defence as the law affords, I have
been and may again be obliged to shield myself
against false charges; for I have no better public
protection. But that a man of keen sensibility
and quick apprehension, whose distinctions and
discriminations are frequently so fine drawn and

so

so shaded that, like colours in the rainbow, their mingled differences cannot be discerned ; that a man who labours to be so cautious in his logic should so often be hurried into the spleen of a cynic, the rashness of a boy, and the petulance of a child, is something extraordinary. There may be many such characters ; but they are seldom so situated as to obtrude themselves, so frequently and forcibly as you have done, into public notice. However, when they do, they are well worthy the attention of the politician, and the philosopher; the man of business, and the man of science.

My purpose in this public address is not to write a libel, or to display my talents for satire. It has a more worthy meaning. It is to warn you and the nation against the effervescence of your passions. The intemperance of public men is tremendously awful at all times; but, when it plunges millions into all the miseries of war, it rises into inexpressible horror. It is strange that, from real benevolence of intention, the mischiefs which fable ascribes to fiends should be the result ! yet this apparent paradox has, of late, been too repeatedly and too woefully proved. You, Sir, and that extrordinary man, Mr. Burke, whose kind but erroneous heart, whose splendid but ill employed talents, have led you astray, are among the examples.

It is my opinion, it is the opinion of thousands,

sands, that you are one of the foremost among those mistaken men, who have brought innumerable miseries upon Europe: and the imminent danger that you may essentially contribute to produce more is the reason of my writing to you. But, Sir, I wish you and my readers carefully to remember that I do not charge you with intentional guilt. It is a thing indeed with which I believe no man can be truly charged : and, in your case, I find abundant proofs that your intentions have been virtuous. It is your ignorance, your errors, your passions, only that are wicked and destructive. You will almost beyond a doubt believe the ignorance, error, passion, and vice to be mine. I cannot help it. I do my duty, by telling some few of those fearful truths with all of which no man is unacquainted, and leave the world to judge of the accuracy of the statement.

Should you ask, " Who, Sir, are you, that dare thus publicly arraign men in 'power, and measures of government?" I answer, I am a man; have a portion of the reasoning faculties of man ; have a feeling of the injuries he suffers; have a prospect of the good he may acquire ; and that I regard all distinctions, except those of morals and of mind, as vicious and absurd.

I have an additional motive, or rather duty : I am one of those " acquitted felons," who, after having been declared innocent by what the

law

law styles their country, seem to be in danger of being voted guilty in the House of Commons. Yes, Sir, I must again assert, I, like you, have my feeling, have a sense of injury, have some principles by which I imagine I can distinguish between right and wrong, and, though I hope I have not the thirst of revenge, I certainly have the desire of justice. The spirit of unrelenting animosity, with which I and my fellow sufferers have been pursued, is so bitter, so absolutely unmixed with any compunctions of benevolence, so disappointed in its appetite for vengeance and blood, and so fanatically pertinacious in continuing its attempts, as to forebode the danger of future scenes, the very aspect of which petrify men with horror. Sir, it is time you should awake! It is time the nation should awake! It is time that the simple truth should be told, without reserve; be the consequences to the teller what they may. Let him but obtain the end he proposes, and if he suffer he will be blest in suffering.

I address myself to you, because your public conduct will be the principal subject of this Letter: and the chief topics I shall have to discuss will be the injustice, the acrimony, and the dangerous tendency, of that conduct; with all which errors I think it teems. It once was asked, Can any good come out of Nazareth? No less incredulous, you too perhaps in a more bitter

tone

tone will demand, Can any good proceed from the heart of a traitor ? The question leads me directly to the point. The memorable words, uttered by you on the first night of the meeting of Parliament, will for ever remain on the records of history; as a proof of the uncharitable, mad, and mischievous spirit, which characterizes the present moment, and present men. All parties have been heated; all perhaps have been more or less mad: but yours, to use a coarse but strong phrase, yours has long been and is stark mad.

"You wished the gentlemen in the minority joy of their exultation, in the innocence of an acquitted felon." You were indignantly called to order (it would have been miraculous if you had not) for having applied the term "felon" to any man, who had been acquitted; and for thus having arraigned and degraded the verdict of an English Jury. You explained, and your commentary did but aggravate the text. A gentleman present, on whose accuracy I can depend, took down your words. "I give the honourable gentlemen joy of their ideas respecting the innocence of persons standing in a situation similar to that of acquitted felons. The felon, when his chains are knocked off, exclaims, with assurance—I am now whitewashed! there has been no legal evidence of my guilt, and I defy any man to say that I am criminal."

B   On

On the fifth of January, you again explained. And how did you explain? You said you never applied the expression [acquitted felon] to the person alluded to; you only meant to say that many of those " who were dismissed from the Old Bailey were such as that House [of Commons] were not bound to think innocent, because the jury had acquitted them ; for many were discharged, not because they were innocent, but, because there was no legal proof of their guilt. Many persons were in this situation, whose real guilt was so notorious that it was hardly denied even by themselves. For this there were various causes: a flaw in the indictment : a misnomer: a defect in legal evidence upon a technical distinction : *or the misunderstanding of the jury.*"

What is it, Sir, that you intend to say ?—— How do you wish to be understood? You and your party affirmed and voted the existence of a conspiracy. You selected me and others as the conspirators. You brought your indictment, in which you asserted our guilt. The jury pronounced us innocent; you repeat your assertions, and pretending to recant, insinuate how they happened so to pronounce: *they wanted understanding.* No flaw, misnomer, or technical defect had been pleaded. Mr. Bonney and Mr. Thelwall might have profited by these legal quirks, but they knew their own innocence and despised

despised them. Technical defects then will not
serve your purpose, and your only refuge is that
a jury does not understand the law. The jury
understood the facts. They could distinguish
between an intention to kill the king and an intention to reform the House of Commons.

Figure to yourself, Sir, the first on the list of
these acquitted felons, Hardy. What were his
views? What his incitements? A man of no
learning, excellent in his morals, simple in his
manners, and, whether they were wise or foolish,
highly virtuous in his intentions. Do you
imagine he meant to make himself prime minister? Were these the marks of a prime minister?
Had he the daring spirit, the deep plans, and
the towering genius of a Cromwell? No one will
affirm things so extravagant. He was a good and
an active man, in his endeavour to procure a parliamentary reform. This he thought, and I
think, would have been the greatest of public
blessings. For this he was tried and declared
NOT GUILTY. The whole country rang with
the verdict, and the affections of the people were
divided, between joy, at his deliverance and
their own, and the contemplation of an innocent
man, who had so long been in danger of the
most dreadful and barbarous death the merciless
law decrees. Compare such a man to an " acquitted felon," who has escaped by the means
you have enumerated : a man who, so far from
exciting the benevolent wishes of a whole people

keeps

keeps all who ever heard his name in a state of dread, lest he should meet them on the highway, or break into their houses by night and murder them in their sleep. Some such action, perhaps many such, he has already committed. At last he is taken; and, knowing no better mode, they hope by his death to be freed from their fears. They are disappointed; a flaw in the indictment, a misnomer, or some technical blunder is committed; he is set free, and they are again subject to his depredations, and to more than all their former terrors; for he has been in prison, where he has infallibly been taught more stratagems, additional daring, and increasing cruelty. Will you affirm, Sir, that there are any common qualities, any kindred sympathies, any moral resemblance, between such a man and Thomas Hardy? A Crown Lawyer, an Alarmist, a Secretary of State, and a Prime Minister, are the only men in the kingdom who would have the effrontery.

Your own commentaries, which I have cited, do but confirm the reprehensible rancour of the phrase, " acquitted felon." You have vainly endeavoured to shew that it had no application, and less meaning. The Solicitor-General and Serjeant Adair, though more guarded in their expressions, have given it a full interpretation. They have maintained the principle in which you were all agreed; but which you, with your usual precipitancy, too broadly published. And what

was

was this principle? It was that men, after their conduct had been scrutinized by every effort which the power of Government could make, which efforts these men were totally incapable of repelling, except by their innocence; after a Secret Committee had sat, and the Alarmists had made their alarming reports; after an extrajudicial bill had been found, against the persons accused, by both Houses of Parliament; after a grand jury had been instructed, in a solemn charge, how they might legally send men to trial on life or death for a conspiracy in supposition, which conspiracy did not exist; after the Solicitor for the Treasury had been authorized farther to instruct this jury how to return a true bill; after the man against whom the heaviest allegations had been brought had endured a trial of eight days, in which means so nefarious and tools so despicable were employed as almost to make Mr. Pitt blush; after a second and a third supposed ringleader had indured scrutinies no less obstinate, though more desponding; after the Right Honourable Mr. Pitt, and his coadjutor, the Most Noble Duke of Richmond, had been compelled to appear and give evidence in favour of the accused, to their mutual and eternal disgrace; after the prevaricating Chancellor of the Exchequer, had denied the recollection of whether he came to a public meeting as a delegate, or from the pure inspirations of patriotic
zeal;

zeal; after he had been awakened from his le-
thargy by the pointed and manly evidence of Mr.
Sheridan, and had made a speech of recantation,
as usual, and a hesitating cowardly avowal of the
truth; after spies, and reports, and private cor-
respondence, and letters purloined, and King's
messengers, and pettyfogging lawyers, and Treasury Solicitors, and Newgate turnkeys, and Bow-
street runners, had all been examined; and, to
sum up the whole, after the persons accused had
been acquitted by an unequivocal and beyond all
example deliberate verdict of Not Guilty, and
the prosecution dropped in despair; still, the
men tried and acquitted, in this extraordinary
and unheard of manner, are pronounced " acquitted felons." This is the unintelligible principle you maintain! Sir, the mind turns with
loathing from the rancour of such an assertion,
the wickednes of such a prosecution, and the errors of such prosecutors. Was it not enough to
have suffered imprisonment, defamation, loss of
property, loss of character, and the hazard of loss
of life? To have been hawked about the streets
like Tyburn malefactors? To have been sung in
ballads as Jacobins and Cannibals? To have been
exhibited on handkerchiefs as traitors, caged in
the cells of Newgate? To have been kept in the
most awful suspence, from the fatal and horrid
sentences that were likely to follow; not because
of our guilt, but of the prejudiced and angry
state

state of the public mind, which had been in-
flamed to this excess by artifices so flagitious and
abominable as these? Could not all this satiate
the fury you had fostered, but you must still pur-
sue us; you must still endeavour, since you
could not hang, to hunt us out of society?
Acquitted felons! Recollect yourself, Sir. I
appeal to your sober moments; or, if sobriety
be quite extinct in you, I appeal to the common
feelings of my countrymen; all of them liable,
as the persons charged with treason have been, to
the pains and penalties that may result from false
accusation; subject to the same calumnies, the
same false imprisonment and the same impossibility of redress; Is this justice? Is it not the
sure token of a mind jaundiced with acrimony
to a dangerous excess?

.Sir, whatever the feelings of the people of
England were before these trials, be assured they
cannot now endure a repetition of such odious
falsehoods. You could not be thus ignorant of
the public sentiment, and, with your burning
haste to do right, you could not be guilty of this
intolerable wrong, were your imagination less
heated, and your intercourse with different ranks
of people more general. You may perhaps,
now and then, hear a solitary dissentient voice;
but you usually mix with men who, like the
parrot educated on board a man of war, can only
repeat the same outrages and the same insults.
You hear nothing else, and nothing else can you
say

say. Would, Sir, you would keep better com-
pany !

The phrase, acquitted felon, you have allow-
ed to be a solecism. I shall therefore only re-
mark, on that head, that solecism is a word
too feeble to characterize its absurdity ; which is
so bare-faced that it could only have been dictated
by a disordered imagination. But against the sentiment it was intended to convey, reason loudly
protests. It is inimical to the general happiness ;
for the general happiness requires that the feelings of man to man should be benevolent, and
that the most persevering inquiries should be
made to discover useful truth ; but that animosities should never be admitted, much less in-
dulged and cherished ; and that punishment,
even according to lawyers themselves, should be
inflicted with the most anxious caution. The
merciful Mr. Serjeant Adair has repeated what
had a thousand times been repeated before :
" That it were better twenty guilty men should
escape, than that one innocent man should suffer." The odious nature of punishment has
indeed always been felt, though the reasons
why it is odious have never been sufficiently
developed.

I have said more than enough on this subject. The feelings of mankind rise in revolt at
the doctrines you, Sir, and your prompters
and defenders preach. Men in general express
the

the highest indignation at them, mingled with the most sovereign contempt. The barbarian bigot, Charlemagne, when he baptized and massacred the four thousand Saxons, was actuated by a kindred spirit. He cut their throats, bade them go to heaven, and thought himself benevolent. He had the power. The imbecile Mitford, the alarmist Adair, the despot Pitt, and your zealous self, have only the will. For this, thanks, blessings, and reverence everlasting be with the Juries.

I shall dismiss the question by adding that there have been splenetic men, reprehensible conduct, and violent expressions, among the friends of reform. Of this I am as deeply convinced as you can be : but there has been no conspiracy. It is in vain, Sir, that you, and the abbettors of your violent measures, assert the contrary. Your own witnesses, three juries, and the general voice and feelings of the nation, have pronounced such affirmations false. They are insulting to common sense.

If other convicted felons resemble me, Sir, you have nothing to fear from their hatred, but much perhaps from their honesty ; for I hold it to be a duty to inquire into the conduct of all men, but particularly of those who undertake to govern and legislate for the whole world ; for whose avaricious grasp three kingdoms were insufficient, whose insatiate ambition the East and the West

c   could

could not glut, but whose triumphal car Europe and all her tributary states must grace. Yes, Sir, I mean to inquire into the acrimony and danger of your public conduct on a more extended scale, than by asking for your proofs of insurrections ; raised, as you have already been told, by an army exercised in a first floor, a camp concealed in a back shop, an arsenal stored with nine muskets, a treasury of almost ten pounds, brass farthings and bad shillings included, and claiming proud support from half a dozen pikes, a host of spies, a couple of clasp knives, and a cavalry cat. Should you be fortunate enough to read with temper, however unjust you may think me for the moment, perhaps you will not read entirely without profit. The soldier who in the heat of battle discovers he has a dangerous wound, if he be not driven quite frantic by the sight of blood, will be desirous of the aid of a surgeon.

A few pages since, I expressed a doubt whether any man can be truly charged with intentional guilt. Let me be more explicit. Men are daily committing actions that are guilty to excess : but they are so absorbed by and intent on self gratification that they have no recollection, at the instant, of the baneful tendency of the crimes they perpetrate. The moment after, perhaps, they awake in all the torments of horror. There are others who begin without principle,

principle, yet have the words integrity, wisdom, and virtue, for ever on their lips. Seeking only to gratify their untutored and selfish desires, they proceed from error to error, and from vice to vice, till the whole is one mass of mischief. The first are fatal, while the tumult of passion rages; which happily is short-lived: but the second meet in council to plan ruin, extend it, and render it permanent There is a third set who are wicked wholly on system; or at least who-mix infinitely less of sense and self; and who therefore entertain the most unshaken conviction that they are systematically wise and good. Conscious of the benevolence of their motives, they admire their worst mistakes the most, and applaud them as the highest virtues. Among the first of these classes robbers and murderers are found; among the second such statesmen as Pitt and Dundas! and among the last philosophers such as yourself and Mr. Burke.

Let me call your attention to some part of the political progress of your passions; the gradations during which you seem to have imbibed a large portion of your present state virtue, and philosophical chivalry.

Beginning only with the first session of the present Parliament, we there find you a firm supporter of Opposition, and the eager friend of inquiring into ministerial delinquency. "To impede inquiry was unconstitutional; and you

asserted

'asserted there was strong ground of suspicion
that it was impeded by Mr. Pitt, because his
conduct could not bear inquiry." This was your
language in Dec. 1790, on Mr. Grey's motion
for the Spanish papers. [See Debrett's Debates,
vol. xxviii. p. 74.]. In this session, you were
the liberal defender of the Catholics, and the
declared foe of Mr. Pitt's artifices of finance.
On the unclaimed dividend bill, you advised the
gentlemen by whom it was supported to consider,
" what they would have thought of it, had such
a bill been proposed by the side of the house on
which you had the honour to sit ? Certain you
were that the right honourable gentleman, who
had moved it, would have poured forth a torrent
of his declamation against it, as a violation of
public faith, a most daring attack on private property, and that the clamour would have been
transmitted from the House to the City, from
the City to the Court, and from the Court to
every corner of the kingdom." [P. 569.]

On the Russian war [April 15, 1791], you
had these remarkable words—" War is a question of great importance to the lives of thousands,
and no man, or member of an assembly, who
decides on it rashly, can think himself free from
guilt. The general sense of the country is
against this war ; and the manufacturers in
many places, and particularly in the city of Norwich, are much alarmed, lest the prosecution of

it

it should bring down irretrievable ruin upon their commerce." [Debates, vol. xxix. p. 174.] How seasonable would such sentiments be at this awful moment? Whenever you spoke on this question, which even then was certainly a great and serious one, you had no mercy on the Minister. At one time, punishment was your theme. [p. 614.] At another, "The right honourable gentleman was placed in the most absurd situation of criminal and accuser." [Vol xxxi, p. 256.] "He was not blamed for having yielded to the public opinion, but for having put himself into such a situation as that he could neither proceed without loss nor retreat without disgrace. The boisterous tones which he had at first assumed, and for which he afterwards substituted the most humiliating concessions, resembled a sudden gust, which terminated in sobs and sighs.—The country had been disgraced and we had incurred the contempt of our enemies and the execration of our allies." [P. 327.] "You called upon those [members] who had refused to exercise their most valuable function of prevention, to exercise that of rigorous inquiry, into a measure which had cost perhaps half a million of the public money; at a time too when they were selling the morals of the people by a lottery." [P. 328.]

At length, Mr. Pitt was so goaded by your attacks that, in the debate on the charge of

corruption

corruption against Mr. Rose, [March 13, 1792]
in reply to your speech, he said that, " though
he had spoken so often, he yet must rise to
justify himself against your inflammatory expressions." And to this defence you again re-
turned a sarcastic and perhaps well merited
reproof. [Vol. xxxii. p. 86.]

Like a wise and virtuous man, you were then
decidedly against lotteries [p. 271] and in favour
of the abolition of the slave trade; on which
last subject you had the following expression.
You asserted that " nations were and ought to
be more bound by morality than individuals."
[P. 400] This, Sir, is a useful and grand
maxim; which, did you but well understand, I
think you must instantly renounce your present
situation, connexions, and pursuits.

Soon after this, the terrors of Mr. Burke
overtook you; and you were seized with the
pangs of indecision. The struggle was violent.
Though a man of much and now and then
perhaps of deep reflection, you still seemed to
be agitated more by contending authorities than
by opposing arguments. Mr. Burke differed
with Mr. Fox, on some essential points. The
breach concerning principles between them was
daily widened; and you hesitated and languished
after both, till you were in danger of agreeing
with neither. What wonder? The genius of
each is towering: but the impassioned flights
of

of Burke were more consonant, to your habits
of mind, than the well digested and simple yet
sublime logic of Mr. Fox. You had indeed
always entertained some part of Mr. Burke's
fears, on the subject of Parliamentary Reform;
and these fears began violently to increase. You
thought " the public mind, both here and in
other countries, was in such a state that even
the slightest scratch might be a mortal wound—
that the beginners of reforms could not always
end them ; and that a temperate parliamentary
reform was impracticable. You alluded to the
doctrines of some of the clubs, that had been
mentioned ; which tended to nothing short of
a total subversion of the constitution. You
recurred to the opinions of our ancestors, and
the veneration in which they held the constitution; among whom the admiration of it was
such that any person, who had uttered a word
of discontent, would either have been supposed
mad or disaffected." [P. 479. April 30, 1792.]

And here, Sir, aware of the personal odium
against myself which I am almost certain to
create, in these times of political superstition,
conscious that I shall again have the cry of Jacobin, Leveller, and perhaps Traitor, echoed
in my ear, I still cannot forbear to suggest how
necessary it is for men to inquire accurately
what they mean, when they speak, in terms
rather of bigotry than of sound understanding,

of

of what they call the constitution. Philosophers
themselves have erected many an imaginary being, each as their idol. They have figured Time,
Space, Motion, Nature, and various other terms
of mere classification, to themselves as real ex-
istences ; and on such assumed data have syste-
matized. Statesmen have followed their example, and Monarchy, Aristocracy, Republic,
Constitution, the Rights of nations, and other
abstract words and phrases, equally denoting
arrangement and relative ideas, have been per-
sonified so often that, at last, they have been
understood, not to signify a number of customs
classed under these different heads, and which
though preserving a degree of resemblance were
continually varying, but each an identical and
permanent existence : a thing perfectly well de-
fined, and which every school-boy could explain ;
so that to ask, What do you mean by Monarchy,
or Republic ? would have been an insult to common sense. I can only say, give to superstition,
religious, philosophic, or political, that which
you imagine to be superstition's due. Let it
endure no persecution. Do you, Sir, as a statesman, worship Baal in your own way. Proclaim the constitution on the high places, in
language as incomprehensible and absolute as
its perfections. Only suffer those, who are not
thus amused by words, to inquire into facts.
What is the Constitution ? Is it a set of unerring

rules,

ules, to make men happy? If you answer,
' No; it is government by King, Lords, and
Commons :" I then ask, Are King, Lords, and
Commons, perfectly virtuous and wise? Should
you reply, " Perfection is not the attribute of
finite beings," the argument must be brought
to this fair conclusion; namely, that which is
imperfect may be better.

If on the contrary you assert its infallibility,
if you tell us in the closet what has so often
been repeated in the senate, that it is a struc-
ture founded on the wisdom of ages, and that
this wisdom was more than human, or almost
more than human; or any other exaggerating
or qualifying epithet, suffer people, who are
but little anxious to differ with you in these
moments of fermenting adoration, to reason
with you the instant you grow cool, and to draw
logical conclusions of the following-kind. Either
this constitution has some virtue in it, which
will guide those who live under its influence to
the best possible state of political and moral
well being, or it has not. If it have this virtue,
the consequences are evident. You are consti-
tutionalists, and all things are in the best of all
possible progress. The present war is a blessing;
the present prime ministers, the present pension-
list, the present House of Commons, the corruptions by which its members obtain their seats,
the national debt and its dreadful increase, the

D   present

present taxes, the inevitable ignorance, miseries
and vices of the poor, the profligacy of the rich,
the pressing of sailors, the kidnapping of soldiers
by arts which all who know and are not actors
in them hold in execration ; these and ten thousand other fearful items are all blessings. If
by constitution you do not, mean this abstract
infallibility, but something that is capable of
amendment, of change, you would then act
wisely to inquire what these possible ameliora-
tions might be ? instead of wasting your time,
like a fanatic, in exalting an incomprehensible
something which you cannot define, which at
the moment you praise your opponents affirm
you infringe, and which, under every possible
supposition, while you stay to adore you neglect
to guard.

This constitution either does or does not re-
late to all the actions of civil society ; it does
or it does not regulate them ; it does or it does
not execute justice in all possible cases. Exert
your faculties, Sir ; think but a little and you
will find that, when we thus amuse ourselves
with words, we act like children. The sole inquiry worthy of man is, What are the best
means of increasing his happiness ? To discover these we must see things as they are,
speak of them as they are, and suffer each other
to shew how we individually suppose they may
become better. However you may deceive
yourself,

yourself, the laws that you and your partisans have made or abrogated, the wars you have excited, the trials you have instituted, and the acrimony you have sowed, have all been directed against this very thing, inquiry, by which alone that public felicity which you imagine you pant to promote can be promoted.

In terror lest the barriers of this all-perfect constitution should be broken down, your abhorrence of innovation and innovators increased apace. That there was danger in the times I will admit; but it was the danger resulting from the asperities and the violence that were practised by the contending parties. It was your misfortune, Sir, however virtuous your intentions might be, to increase the evil which you wanted the wisdom to redress. Imbibing the unhappy and half frantic zeal of Mr. Burke, you daily departed farther from your former principles and companions. You rose, trembling, with the ardour of conversion and the fear of defeat, to reply to Mr. Fox.. The Chancellor of the Exchequer was no longer the butt at which you aimed the shafts of ridicule and the glances of contempt. Though at first you could not praise, you declaimed on the prudence of supporting him. You continued to sit with the Opposition, while your friendship for their cause was nightly on the decline. Bickerings and bitter feelings, though clouded under con-

fused

fused explanatary phrases, each time you spoke
recurred. Your principles underwent a remarkable change. On Friday January 4, 1793,
you supported Ministry on the question of the
Alien bill. You declaimed on the danger of
removing any Minister, good or bad. After
supposing hypothetically, and not *then* as an
opinion of your own, " that a better Administration *might* be formed, yet you would not
vote for its change." Nay you even asserted
that an " Administration being a bad one was a
reason why, at that time, you would not attempt
to remove them : because, in proportion as they
might be bad, would they *by all means* strive to
remain in power : *to the neglect and detriment of
the public business.*" You have lived, Sir, to see
this maxim fulfilled ; ay and, however unconsciously, to act upon it. You admired this
Alien bill ; you approved the proclamations, de-
fended the calling out of the militia, affirmed
the existence of insurrections, and were among
the most panic-struck of the Alarmists. The
suspension of the act of Habeas Corpus, the
declaration by the Commons of the existence of
a dangerous conspiracy, the virulent assertions
and puerile reports of the Secret Committee, the
illegal examinations of suspected men before the
Privy Council, their commitment and the prosecutions instituted against them for high treason, all had your open and ardent support.; all
were

were excited by you with a degree of rashness of which you could not have been guilty, had you been aware of its consequences.

The intemperance of your party, (And who among them, Sir, has been more intemperate than yourself ?) bred such confusion in their plans that they knew not how to relinquish them, or how to proceed. To-day they met to interrogate men who would give no answer, to train and to regulate spies, and to discover or to create traitors. To-morrow they would be employed in new modelling their distracted Cabinet, disposing of marquisates, blue-ribbands, and viceroyships, grasping at sinecures, and wrangling in a very chaos of selfish-broils, dark intrigues, and tormenting jealousies. The next day they would assemble with woe-begone aspect, and sit waiting for the advice of him who best could tell how to announce to the nation the capture of cities, the loss of provinces, the ruin of armies, and the shameless defection of venal Allies. They had but one solace ; they met at ministerial dinners ; where, pretending to forget or to smother their mutual animosities, they drank oblivion to their cares, perdition to their opponents, and applauded him most whose frenzy or whose falsehood could assert that the nation was victorious, that the French were detestable wretches, carmagnoles, and cannibals, and on the eve of being exterminated, and that whoever thought differently

rently

rently were Jacobin villains, for whom hanging would be too merciful. Yes, Sir, you now form a part of that Administration, who are striving *by all means* to remain in power ; *to the neglect and detriment of the public business.*

Sir, I will do you justice : you have intended to save the state ; and the more you have felt your passions rise the more you have been convinced of the purity of your motives, and the success of your plans. You mistook anger for energy, and virulence for virtue. You erroneously supposed that hatred for what you thought vice was wisdom, and punishment prevention. Alas, Sir, it is these mistakes, these pernicious maxims, that have plunged all Europe into horrors till now unheard of! And it is a melancholy truth that in producing these horrors, though seeking to avert them, you have had your full share. Your agency has been open and unremitting, your enmity avowed, and in proportion as your rash counsel has proved abortive, your choler has increased. The fermentations of passion never were and never can be wise or virtuous. Anger is too blind to prevent evil, too headstrong to be warned of it, and too precipitate to produce good. You, Sir, have been permanent in anger ; and the consequences are such as your more dispassionate former friends have uniformly predicted ; fatal to your own peace, and destructive to the nation.

The

The excess to which this acrimony has been carried is as amazing as it is lamentable. In the venom of vengeance, with which Alarmists have been devoured, no language could express its corrosive antipathies. Levellers, villains, fire-brands, traitors, every epithet that could give vent to the bursting gall of passion has been but common place. Sir, if there have been fire-brands, you and the men you now style your noble and right honourable friends - will be ranked in the annals of history as the chief. If there have been traitors, you and your official co-partners are they. It is you that conspire, however unconsciously, against the throne you revere, and the people you pretend to protect. Of all other dangers, the danger of that viru-lence in which you indulge is the greatest. It is pregnant with ruin to all part'es, but most to your own.

Who is it that really inflame the minds of the people ? Those who drag the brothers, sons, and husbands of the poor to slaughter ? or those whose peaceful principles are incessantly strug-gling to protect and save them ? Those who by every artifice set brother against brother, arm man against man, and with the restlessness fa-bulously ascribed to fiends leave no angry pas-sion unmoved, no hateful violence untried, to spread wide and wider the dreadful havoc they have begun ? or those who, with no less ardour,

labour

labourto calm the spirit of rage, appease the con-
flagration of the passions, and bid the horrible
ruin subside ?

Would I had the gift of persuasion ! Would
I had the power to state a few indisputable and
acknowledged truths in all their simplicity, and
all their force ! Then should I convince you, and
all mankind, that war, persecution, and hatred,
must everlastingly and under all possible circumstances be destructive. They never had, nor
ever can have, any other origin than the irra-
tional and ruinous effervescence of the passions ;
and, when the passions subside, they can no
longer exist. To incite millions of men to murder one another, and to pretend that this is for
their mutual happiness, is a propositon too extravagant and absurd for language to express. The
plea of ignorance only can be urged in behalf of those
who maintain such monstrous assertions. To en-
force the necessity of self defence, to talk of the
honour of the nation and the impossibility of
peace, are fallacies which, however wise and good
men of all parties may be amused by them, are as
pernicious as they are childishly ridiculous.
Who is the nation ? Or, granting this abstract
term to be a real existence, what can so truly
personify it as the general happiness ? Can stabs
with the bayonet, can limbs blown from the body
by gunpowder, can brains scattered by cannon
balls, can the agonies of ten thousand men, op-
pressing

pressing the bare earth with horror, staining the ri-
vulets with blood, writhing, groaning, and dying,
can the inclemencies of the sky, the damps of
marshes, the agues, fevers, and consumptions of
unsheltered ditches, can pestilence, fire, frost, and
famine, increase the sum of human happiness?
Surely the time will come when men will never
again maintain doctrines so diabolic, so mischievous, so mad, so abhorredly repugnant as
well to reason as humanity. This philosophy?
This good government? This for a people's
happiness? Grant me patience while I recollect
the frenzy of the human race! This for a nation's honour? Common sense spurns and sickens
at such abominable assertions.

Again: granting this multiform being, this
creature called Nation, to be a reality: What is
that other creature, called its Honour? How much
of the honour of the first of June appertains to
the sailor who lighted the match that sunk the
French ship, Le Vengeur? Would it not be as
rational to inquire how much of the guilt? Poor
wretch! He knew not what he was doing. By
a turn of the wrist, he sent full twelve hundred
souls, possessed by heroism unequalled since the
days of Leonidas, shouting as they sunk in the
same mistaken spirit, *for their nation's honour*, all
to the bottom. Let them sink! Were they not
French dogs? It was for the *honour of Old England*; and he could shout when they could be

E   heard

heard no more. The actors of Drury Lane, and
the tumblers of Sadler's Wells, have acted these
honours. They have opened schools to infuri-
ate mankind, and propagate a brood of heroes;
and the sinking of ships and the slaughter of
their brothers were the topics of vapouring and
insult, of ballad singing and Bartholomew fair
ribbaldry, of crackers and illuminations, all for
the National Honour! Be it so; but let those
who use and understand the terms know that I
am not one of any such Nation; and, if these
are its honours, that I hold its honours in abhorrence.

What can be said? Is this the age of Reason?
Exert yourselves, summon your fortitude, ye
lovers of truth, proclaim her benevolent tenets,
promulgate her peaceful precepts, or the age of
Reason will never be here. Seek no personal
vengeance, be guilty of no intentional insult, but
declare your thoughts; and if persecution come,
because you have openly and honestly warned
men against their errors, give it welcome. Having accused without malice, suffer without com-
plaint. Persevere, and in life or in death you
will receive and communicate happiness.

Lost in the immensity of thoughts so over-
whelming, is it wonderful, Sir, that I should
have forgotten you? Well, honour was the question; and, since men will thus bewilder themselves in words, we must talk their own dialect.

Know

Know then, Sir, that those who speak the unqualified language of the angry world, and particularly of your party, affirm that the persons who proclaim themselves the guardians of this phantom of a phantom, this National Honour, have officially employed every degree of perfidy, from the Spy to the Despot, that they could devise, and every species of venality, ruinous and ridiculous, from the full treasury to the empty blue ribband, which the little cunning they had could suggest, to its everlasting disgrace. If these assertions are false, at least they are common ; and have every semblance of truth. The names of Lynam, Groves, Alexander, and Taylor, are as certainly on record as those of Frederic, Francis, and Catharine. The three guineas, to bear the travelling charges of each of the sturdy Sheffield witnesses, will as surely appear, in the account books of the Exchequer, as will the six millions ; which, if we are mad enough, we have now a glorious and honourable opportunity to bestow, or lend.

And to whom ? To an Emperor ! Can an Emperor be poor ? Can an Emperor borrow money of traders ? Dealers in raw hides, hemp, and hob-nails ? Degrading thought ! Cannot his title make money, conjure up men, and command plenty from the seasons, and prosperity to all his wishes ? It were blasphemy, against the sacred dignity of sound, to suppose such imbecility ! And, were the libeller

within

within the flight of the Imperial eagle, so he should find. Sir, neither the charms of title nor the incantations of honour will raise from the dead the miriads that lie, buried in the fields of France, the forests of Germany, the sands of Spain, the mountains of Italy, and the morasses of Belgium. Racking recollection ! Horrible thought ! Of these the promoters of this most sanguinary of wars have been the murderers. The mischief now can have no remedy : but it might instantly have an end.

Wretched, ill-fated Poland ; miserable people; victims of perfidy, for which the annals of vice have no parrallel ! Shall your groans die away with the passing breeze ? Shall your tears wash the guilt of your oppressors to oblivion ? Shall your blood fertilize your usurpers fields, yielding joy to the barbarian usurpers ? Never ! Hemlock and the deadly nightshade shall be their fruits ! In the intrails of such inhuman butchers, grain the most wholesome and pulse, the most nutritive shall only corrode and kill ! Touched by them, milk and honey shall turn to gall, the blind worm and toad shall infest their paths, and vipers shall start wherever they tread ! Detestable monsters ! My soul shudders at your infernal deeds, and Reason herself half delights in hating you ! Yes, she will pardon this rhapsody ; for she feels that she has no words to express the heart-rending sensations you excite.

Perhaps,

Perhaps, Sir, you will ask, " What have I to
do with Russian cruelties, or Polish miseries?"
To questions other questions are frequently the
best answer. The Poles have long been a suffer-
ring race. Had equity been the grand mover of
states, they must long since have met with protection. That protection, I am convinced, need
not have been war. But, since statesmen at present understand no better means, what, Sir, if
you and the counsellors of the English Cabinet
had been equally urgent, in your advice, to
combine the nations of Europe in favour of a
people afflicted and preyed upon by surrounding
despots, instead of turning your arms against a
state that was labouring in the pangs and throes
of infant liberty? If you must reform kingdoms by carnage, terror, and devastation, were
there no abuses to reform there where men are
bought and sold like cattle? Could not the mas-
sacre at Ismail move you? Is there nothing of-
fensive to your feelings in the wantonly infernal
murder of the twelve thousand unarmed inha-
bitants of Praga? Have you read the Russian
state paper; in which the cities sacked, the provinces laid waste, the slaughter committed, the
seizure of a kingdom, and the confirmed slavery
of a nation struggling for freedom, are exult-
ingly recapitulated; and the whole glory of
deeds, at which devils would tremble, ascribed to the immediate interposition of the
Deity?

Deity? A being supposed to be all perfect;
all wise; all merciful; to whom injustice is
impossible; and who, having wearied himself with fighting for his beloved Russians,
reposes in delight to hear his blood hounds chaunt
Te Deum! The soul sickens at such pernicious,
such gross, such impudent absurdities! Sir,
they will not, they cannot be much longer endured. I know not what effect such thoughts
may, at present, produce on a mind like yours.
There was a time when the same events would
have given birth to emotions so violent in you as
to have rendered it necessary to cool your feelings, before you attempted to express them;
lest they should have seemed like the effusions of
frenzy. How you acquired your present philosophic apathy, on such subjects, I leave you to
explain.

There was a time, too, when you were beloved by your constituents; when you were
alarmed at the very prospect of a war with this
Russia; a country so distant that, compared
with the present war, it would have been fighting with the sword in the scabbard. Norwich
was a principal object of your anxiety; and the
" irretrievable ruin of its commerce" a consequence which you foresaw, and at which you
shuddered. How strangely absurd are the ebul-
litions of passion For surely, Sir, you cannot
pretend that you were in your sober senses, when

you

you asked, on the 30th of December, " Who
could say that he had felt the war? When you
would demand, " Had any man in that house,
felt its distresses? Had the poor felt them?"—
Sir, the warmest of your partisans shrunk back
and blushed, at the rash intemperance of your
zeal. What! Has no man in the nation felt
this war? Not the poor themselves! I will suppose the rich to have but little feeling; not because they are not men and capable of all good:
but because, by the unhappy institutions of society, they are perverted men; but, at a time
when the poor are dragged to the slaughter-
house by thousands; when the orphan and the
widow are left to perish for want of support;
when most of the manufacturers in the kingdom,
except those who prepare the implements of de-
struction, are either entirely out of employ or
reduced to half work, or half pay; when the
first necessaries of life, even bread, potatoes,
and coals, are rising to double their accustomed
value; when the rich themselves deem it necessary to be parsimonious, and the fine arts are all
languishing and ready to expire; when a national debt, dreadful to contemplate, has brought
with it a load of taxes that oppress the powers
of the whole people, vigorous as they have been;
and when no less a sum than twenty-four millions is again demanded for the increase of that
intolerable debt; at such a moment, in times so

full

full of terror and dismay, will men suffer to be
told that the war is not felt? Is it possible that
a pervertion of truth and reason so incredible as
this can be real?

And how is it, at present, with your once
loved city of Norwich? I have written to inquire; and this is the information I have receiv-
ed, from a gentleman whose intercourse in society
is great, his research zealous, and his communica-
tions from the first source.

" There can be no doubt of the distress of
the poor in this city. A comber, who used to
employ sixty men, now is able to employ only
fifteen. A hotpresser, whom I know, assured
me that all the hotpressers in this city do not
now employ so many journeymen as he alone
did, before the war. The money paid, to the
villages in the country for spinning, before the
war, was a thousand pounds per week. It is at
this time not quite half the sum ; and the quantity of spinning that used to be done for one
shilling is now done for sixpence; so that the
poor spinners are doubly distressed. I do not
find that the price of either combing or weaving
is reduced; there is only a less quantity re-
quired.

The printed account of the receipts and disbursements, of the Court of Guardians of the
City of Norwich, from April 1st 1793 to
April 1st 1794, states the disbursements to
have

have been 22,659l. 6s. 5d. The out-door allowances solely to the poor were 7,327l. 9s. 11d.
and another correspondent adds, in a manuscript
note—" The out-door allowances will be one-
" third more next quarter. 1500l. were sub-
" scribed last week, to distribute coals and bread
" for a week or two, in addition to the out-
" door allowance."

Of the same correspondent I had inquired,
concerning the real state of the poor at Norwich;
and, exclusive of the above intelligence, the
following was the answer—" The poor rates,
" which used to be one shilling and ninepence
" in the pound per quarter, are now four shil-
" lings and ninepence; and are expected to be
" six shillings next quarter, and to go on increas-
" ing. There is scarcely any work in the town,
" and a poor industrious manufacturer said to
' me"—" I am like a bird in the field : when I
' have got one meal, I am forced to seek abroad
' for another.'

How many towns and cities are in the same
situation? And will you still persist in affirm-
ing, Sir, that the war is not felt by the poor?
I am far from applauding curses, or any other
expressions of anger and revenge; but if they
exist it is not my fault, and the people of Norwich, in the bitterness of their hearts, some and
indeed the most part for the immediate distresses
brought upon them by this war, and others be-

cause

cause of your political desertion, the people of
Norwich invoke curses on your name. I hope
they will learn to be more benevolent, and to
oppose and detect your measures and mistakes,
yet do justice to the integrity of your heart.
But your conduct there, Sir, especially on your
late election, was so full of that acrimony and
passion of which I have been accusing it that,
should they take the moral advice which I have
just given them, they would certainly act very
contrary to any thing that could be expected
from you in return.

Electioneering arts, at best, too fatally de-
monstrate the corruptions of our present system :
but even these are odious in degree; and some
infinitely more so than others. A loom in
mourning was carried in procession, by the
friends of your opponent; and the effect it pro-
duced, on the distressed manufacturers, was
such as might well be expected, but such as
you could not endure. You immediately or-
dered one of the most disgusting spectacles
that the human imagination could frame: though
I grant that the same detestable artifice had
been employed, in every variety, to enflame
the populace of London. You went to a car-
penter, in person, and directed him to make a
guillotine; and to place a female figure, on the
platform of the horrid instrument, with its
head in the act of being struck off, and bleeding ;

ing : over which was an inscription, in large letters, THIS IS FRENCH LIBERTY ! An artifice, Sir, so full of passion, and of so disgusting and enflaming a nature, was, I believe, never employed before, on such an occasion. Charles Fox, holding the gore dripping head of the late King of France by the hair; Mr. Sheridan feasting with him, at a banquet of decapitated kings; monstrous figures of pretended Frenchmen, devouring the bodies of their murdered fellow citizens ; and other infernal devices, had insulted the feelings of the citizens of London, in every print-shop : but no man, perhaps, except yourself, would at a popular election, when party heats and feuds are so violent and so dangerous, thus have been blind to and regardless of their dreadful consequences. They were immediately foreseen by an active though prudent gentleman, who was the friend of Mr. Mingay. I speak, Sir, from authority. He went to the Sheriffs and requested them, as peace officers, to prevent the procession of this hateful and dangerous guillotine. He could not, he said, answer for the consequences; which probably would end in riot. You were present, and exclaimed, " Well, Sir, we are ready to meet you, on that ground. If you have a mind to try your strength, let us *fight it out !*" It was fortunate that your opponent was a man of some temper ; and from him your angry spirit met well merited reproof.

He

He could not however prevent all the mischief
he foreboded. You led your guillotine and
bleeding figure in procession; but its triumph
was of short duration. Your opponent's party,
indignant at its appearance and regardless of
personal safety, rushed into the adverse crowd and
in an instant shivered the pageant to atoms. I dis-
approve the action, but I state the fact. It proves
that your challenge to *fight it out* was like your
political actions in general, a bravado. What,
Sir, shall the man who has been instigating
prosecutions for a conspiracy to rise in tumult
and depose the king, shall he be the first to
encourage insurrection? If there have been
treason, who are the traitors? Who are the
exciters to civil contention, and pell-mell havoc?

Do you remember, Sir, a poor manufacturer of
the name of Amis? This man (my correspondent had the tale from his own lips) thinking you
had not kept faith with him, because you had
injured instead of protected the trade of Norwich,
went into the Angel Inn yard in that city, to
wait for you. When you appeared, he advanced,
and reminded you of the promise you had made
him, at the last election; and of his having
voted for you, in consequence of that promise.
Fearful perhaps of speaking too plainly, he
couched his phrase in a kind of election joke.—
" I doubt, Sir, said he, you were a little ro-
guish,

guish, at that time of day. But I must tell you that our trade has been hurt, for want of proper protection, and a safe convoy. And now, Sir, you have voted for the war: so you have not kept your word." You replied : " This is not a time to talk of these things." " It is the only time I can take," answered Amis. " I may not see you again for many months; and I must tell you my mind."—" You may go and be damned, all of you," was the answer of the statesman and philosopher Mr. Windham ! Nor was this all your philosophy : you raised your arm, as if intending to strike the man ; but the less choleric bye standers interposed. You then called for the constables, to clear the yard of the crowd ; for it was full of people. This account Amis, in his simple but honest phraseology, says " he would swear to, before the greatest " king in the world."

These, Sir, are not the fictions of my brain. I had heard numerous flying reports of your vehement conduct, during your late election, of the authenticity of which I wanted proof. This induced me to seek correspondents, on whose veracity I could depend ; being convinced that, if the reports were true, they ought to be made public. The facts I have written were sent me, in answer to the questions I asked ; and the per-sons who gave me the information pledge them-

selves

selves to their having inquired with accuracy and reported with fidelity.

. Every part of your present conduct agrees with the rest, and I am truly amazed at the blindness which fear, faction, and office have created ! This war not felt by the poor ? When was there a war in which its miseries and its burthens were not supported by them ? When was there a war, of two years, so oppressive and teeming with misery as the present ? Under the most favourable circumstances, what is the condition of the poor ? You are a statesman ; do you not know ? I will not suppose you are to be taught that the tillage of the land, and the labour bestowed upon its products, constitute the whole wealth of men. Who are the tillers ? Who are the manufacturers ? The poor. Without their labour, the earth itself would be barren. The foundation of the laws of property is that each man is affirmed to be entitled to the produce of his own industry. If these original laws therefore were executed, with all the rigour with which it is pretended they ought to be observed, the poor and the poor only would be entitled to eat ; for it is their labour alone that produces food. For this labour, what do the rich give them in return ? Oppression, insult, contempt. Of the only thing which could conduce to their happiness, knowledge, they are debarred ;

barred ; by the continual drudgery to which they are subjected. Examine for a moment the relative situation, between them and their taskmasters. Who make the laws? The rich— Who alone can with probable impunity break the laws ?—The rich—Who are impelled by want and misery to break them, and afterward are imprisoned, transported, and hanged ?—The poor.—Who do the work ?—The poor.—Who reap the fruits ?—The rich.—Who pay the taxes ?—The poor; for their labours pay every thing.—Who impose the taxes ? — The rich, whose luxury devours what the labours of the poor produce.—On what do the rich feed ?— On the product of the poor's misery.—On what do the rich ride ?—On the bent and half-broken back of the poor.—What supports the fine houses, parks, and palaces, of the rich ?—The hunger and thirst of the poor.—With what do they purchase their gaudy carriages ; fit only to engender disease and indolence ; in which they loll, look down on and drive over the industrious man on foot ?—With the price of wretchedness, paid by the poor.—On what do the rich revel and riot, make feasts, and routes, and encourage gaming, gluttony, drunkenness, and every species of vice ?—On the groans and tears and sweat and blood of the poor.—For what do the rich quarrel ?—For the groans and tears and sweat

and

and blood of the poor.—Have not the rich clubs, night meetings, and societies?—The rich have public brothels; where they are guilty of practices such as none but appetites the most detestable and depraved could endure. They have gaming-houses; where they have frequently been known to stake the day's labour of half a million of men on a single card, or dice : and they have clubs, in which politicians meet ; to consult how they may trick one another, buy rotten boroughs, and secure to themselves the fruit of the labour which they lay on the shoulders of the poor.—And do no justices, no constables, no lord mayors, interfere?—No : they say what they please, do what they please, and publish what they please against each other, and provided they do not attack the craft, on which they all fatten — Why are the rich proud, and arrogant, and insolent ? — Because the poor are ignorant, and distressed, and heart-broken.—Why do the rich treat the poor with contempt ?—Because the poor must either bend or starve.—Why are the rich tyrants ?—Because the poor are humbled, and terrified till they dare not speak.

Prove, Sir, if you can, that there is exaggeration in any one of these assertions. I speak from deliberate reflection, and affirm that I think I can defy you.

From the same deliberate examination, I do

most sincerely and from my soul believe, you
would be among the first to alleviate the present
miseries of the poor, and aid in their future felicity, did you know the means : and that you
would be no less zealous to do as much good to
the nation and to mankind as you have contri-
buted to do harm, but from the impediments
arising from ignorance. Ignorance is the source
of your impotence. Ignorance is the origin
of all the errors of which I or the world can ac-
cuse you. To attribute the mischief of which
the most pernicious of men are guilty to any
other cause, whether to their delight in malice
the vice inherent in their nature or any imaginary constitutional defect whatever, is the reason
of all our uncharitableness, and want of urba-
nity. But, though the knowledge of this truth
would induce me to serve and never to injure the
worst man on earth, it must not lead me, in for-
bearance to the individual, to neglect my duty to
the whole. My intention has not been to
wound, but to awaken, to warn, and if possible
to shorten those woes with which the arrogance
and errors of men are afflicting the earth. In
declaring this, I make no apology ; for I must
not apologize for having discharged a duty. I
only wish to avoid giving activity to a vice,
which I have been condemning ; the vice of
anger; the irritability, passion, and rash conduct
to which you are so remarkably subject. I

' G   have

have uttered the dictates of an honest, a well meaning heart. Should you attribute motives the very reverse to me, I shall remain unmoved; and shall reply it was rather your misfortune than your fault that you did not understand me better.

THOMAS HOLCROFT.

P. S. The party with which you act have been repeatedly and truly charged with reviling the French, and then imitating them : the following quotation, from the famous speech of Lord Mornington, page 47 [printed for Debrett] if compared with your suspension bill and treasonable prosecutions, will afford a most odious and revolting instance of imitation.

' This decree of the Convention was proposed ' expressly for the purpose of punishing'— " not traitors only, but even those who dared " to be indifferent to the cause of the existing " government; who had the audacity to be pas- " sive.—Such persons must be governed by *the* " *sword*, since it was impossible to govern them " *by the maxims of justice.*"

www.ingramcontent.com/pod-product-compliance
Lightning Source LLC
Chambersburg PA
CBHW030903260626
47169CB00008B/2667